Da Wei's Treasure

A Chinese Tale

retold by MARGARET and RAYMOND CHANG

Illustrated by LORI McELRATH-ESLICK

MARGARET K. McELDERRY BOOKS

In memory of my mother
—R. C.

To my mom, with love
—L. M. E.

Also by MARGARET AND RAYMOND CHANG

THE BEGGAR'S MAGIC
illustrated by David Johnson

IN THE EYE OF WAR

THE CRICKET WARRIOR
illustrated by Warwick Hutton

(MARGARET K. MCELDERRY BOOKS)

Margaret K. McElderry Books
An Imprint of Simon & Schuster Children's Publishing Division
1230 Avenue of the Americas
New York, NY 10020

Text copyright © 1999 by Margaret and Raymond Chang
Illustrations copyright © 1999 by Lori McElrath-Eslick

Book design by Michael Nelson

The text of this book was set in Weiss.
The illustrations were rendered in oil.

Printed in Hong Kong
First Edition
10 9 8 7 6 5 4 3 2 1

LIBRARY OF CONGRESS CATALOGING-IN-PUBLICATION DATA
Chang, Margaret Scrogin.
Da Wei's treasure: a Chinese tale / retold by Margaret and
Raymond Chang ; illustrated by Lori McElrath-Eslick.
—1st ed.   p.   cm.
Summary: In this retelling of a traditional Chinese tale,
a boy finds a treasure in an unexpected place.
ISBN 0-689-81835-1 [1. Folklore—China.] I. Chang, Raymond.
II. McElrath-Eslick, Lori, ill. III. Title. PZ8.1.C3584Daw 1998
398.2'0951'02—dc21 [E]   97-26848

FIRST
EDITION

Once, a long time ago, a widowed peasant and his son, Da Wei, lived in a village in northern China. The climate was harsh, so they had to work long hours to survive. Their landlord was the local Magistrate, and he demanded a large part of their harvests.

Poor though they were, father and son took care of each other. Every evening, Da Wei prepared nourishing soup while his father rested. Every night after supper, the old man sat beside the oil lamp and taught Da Wei to read and write.

"We may be poor peasants," Da Wei's father said, "but we should not be ignorant."

Their small cottage contained one treasure: a large rock, shaped like a mountain, that had come from deep in the ocean. The rock was a gift from a lonely old fisherman whom Da Wei's father had looked after when he was young. He kept it on the floor in the corner of the kitchen, where he would often sit staring at it.

Green moss softened the rock's craggy surface. Small holes opened like windows from its dark center. A miniature house stood on top of the rock, and a tiny, graceful tree grew beside it. Sometimes clouds drifted out of the holes. Then Da Wei's father would say, "Rain is coming soon." He was always right.

After years of hard work and poverty, Da Wei's father lay in bed, gravely ill.

"You are a fine son, honest and hardworking," the old man whispered to Da Wei, who sat beside him. "I am sorry that all I can leave you is the rock. Keep it safe, for the fisherman said that one day a light would shine from the house, and the rock would show the way to treasures deep beneath the sea."

Da Wei tucked the ragged coverlet around his father. "Don't talk. Rest," he said.

"No, I must tell you this." His father spoke slowly, with great effort. "When you were born, the fortune-teller said that you were destined for a happy life. Perhaps you will find the treasure."

Later that night, the old man died.

For a long time after that, Da Wei worked the land alone. At night, when he was not worn out, he would read a poem or practice calligraphy, remembering his father.

One night, Da Wei woke suddenly, dreaming of flute music. Light glimmered in the hallway. Thinking he had forgotten to blow out the oil lamp, he went into the kitchen. The windows of the miniature house blazed with light.

Da Wei waited, hardly daring to breathe. Suddenly, the door of the house swung open, and a tiny black cart rolled out. Da Wei held out his hand to catch it and gently placed it on the floor beside the rock. The light in the house went out. Da Wei waited in the dark kitchen, but nothing more happened. At last he went back to bed.

By morning, the cart had grown big enough for Da Wei to use. Just as he was wondering how he could get it through the door, the cart rolled across the kitchen, pulled in its sides, and slipped out into the garden. There it stood, waiting for him. It was indeed a farmer's treasure, for it rolled easily over bumpy paths and made the heaviest loads seem light. It could stand in the rain for hours but never get wet.

Months later, after Da Wei had gathered the summer harvest, he decided to visit the seaside village where his father had met the old fisherman. He took the cart with him. During the three-day journey, he begged for his food and slept under the cart.

At last, Da Wei reached a hill overlooking the vast ocean. He spread his arms wide to catch the sea wind, awed by the sound of waves. Before he could stop it, the cart rolled down the hill, across the beach, and into the surf. The great waves parted before it, opening a dry path that beckoned Da Wei under the sea.

Da Wei grasped the cart's handles and trotted along as it rolled forward. He looked straight ahead, but out of the corners of his eyes he could see walls of water rising on either side, and, beyond the walls, fish swimming.

The path led to the gate of a magnificent mansion. Laughter rose from inside. As he approached, the gate swung open, and he entered. The walls of water vanished, and Da Wei seemed to be on dry land once more.

He had never before seen a house this grand. Its beams and doors were of polished redwood, and its roof tiles were made of blue porcelain. Bright flowers filled the garden. Several young girls tossed a ball in the courtyard, while puppies and kittens scampered around their feet.

The girls paid no attention to Da Wei, and he was too shy to speak to them. Only one small orange kitten greeted him, mewing and rubbing against his legs.

Trembling with curiosity and fear, Da Wei left the cart in the courtyard and entered the mansion. He found a sumptuous meal waiting for him in an empty room. When he called out, no one answered. The kitten looked at him and looked at the table, as if telling him to eat.

Da Wei was hungry, so he filled his rice bowl, took large helpings of tender prawns and fish in a savory sauce, and drank several cups of fragrant, soothing tea. His hunger satisfied, he wandered down the hallway into a book-lined study. A brazier of burning coals warmed the room, and a comfortable chair invited him to sit and read a book of poems. Exhausted by his journey, he soon fell fast asleep.

When he woke, dusk had fallen. Lighted lanterns swung from the ceiling. The vast mansion stood silent and empty, except for the kitten curled up on his lap. Frightened, Da Wei held the kitten in his arms and went back to the courtyard. The gate swung open, and the path between the cliffs of water led back to the distant shore.

Da Wei followed it, still holding the kitten. The gate swung shut. Only then did Da Wei remember that he had left the cart inside. But it was too late. Da Wei could hear the walls of water collapsing behind him. He dared not look back. He ran ahead and soon reached the shore.

The kitten turned out to be a far greater treasure than the lost cart. Every evening when Da Wei came home from the fields, he found her waiting for him. When he practiced calligraphy, she sat on the table, watching every stroke intently. When he read a poem aloud, she would purr, as if admiring its beauty. He was no longer lonely.

One evening, a delicious aroma greeted Da Wei as he walked toward his house. He found the soup he had prepared earlier simmering on the stove, the table neatly laid, the house tidy, his clothes washed and mended. The kitten sat contentedly on the windowsill, her paws tucked under her chest.

After supper, he asked his neighbors if they had seen anyone enter his house. "No, no one," each neighbor said.

The next evening, the house had been carefully cleaned, and he found a small, plucked game bird and vegetables from his garden lying ready to cook. Placed beside them on the table was a pillow cover made of old silk, exquisitely embroidered with designs of fish and sea plants. From the windowsill, the kitten watched him cook his supper.

The next afternoon, Da Wei left his field work early. Quietly, he approached his house.

An orange kitten skin lay on the windowsill. Through the window, Da Wei could see a young woman sitting, intent on her embroidery.

Da Wei crept up to the window and snatched the skin. The young woman stood up, startled.

"Who are you?" Da Wei asked in wonder.

The young woman put down her embroidery and came to face Da Wei. "Once, I was the Second Mistress of Embroidery in the Jade Emperor's court," she answered. "The First Mistress was so jealous of my skill that she spilled ink on a silk gown I was embroidering for the Jade Empress. I was blamed, and the Emperor sent me to live as a kitten in that mansion under the sea."

Da Wei listened in astonishment, hardly daring to believe that the girl who stood in his poor cottage had once belonged to the heavenly court of the Jade Emperor.

"Why did you leave the undersea mansion to come with me? I—I'm so poor," he stammered.

"There, I would have been a kitten forever. I chose to become a mortal woman on Earth." She smiled at Da Wei. "And you looked kind."

Da Wei gathered his courage and asked her to marry him. She consented, and told him her name, Lian Di. From then on, his house was full of laughter.

Lian Di's embroidered silk fetched high prices on market day. Word of her skill spread throughout the province. Wealthy families clamored for her elegant garments. She bought a loom with her earnings and wove fine, shimmering silk. In a year, she had earned enough money to buy farmland with fertile soil. There they built a bigger house.

The local Magistrate was a greedy and corrupt man. When he realized that Da Wei would no longer lease his land, he summoned Da Wei to his court and said, "How could a poor peasant like you get rich so fast? You must have robbed someone. Or maybe you murdered a rich man."

The Magistrate had Da Wei arrested and put in jail. He demanded a huge fine, more than Da Wei could afford.

Lian Di visited her husband in jail that night. She brought him food and a little tiger cut out of paper. "Keep this with you," she whispered. "Don't be afraid tomorrow, whatever your sentence. Just repeat these words: 'Your Honor is talking nonsense.'"

Da Wei wept as they parted, for he was sure he would never see her again.

The next morning, Da Wei was chained and taken into the courtroom. The Magistrate asked, "Are you ready to confess and pay your fine?"

When Da Wei said he did not have the money, the Magistrate ordered the guards to cane him twenty times. Da Wei shouted that he was innocent, but no one listened. Then he uttered the words Lian Di had taught him: "Your Honor is talking nonsense. Your Honor is talking nonsense."

The paper tiger leaped out of his pocket and grew into a giant tiger, with sharp teeth and claws and flames coming out of its mouth and nostrils. It roared and jumped at the Magistrate. The flames set his clothes on fire and burned his long beard. He ran from the courthouse yelling for mercy. The tiger caught up with him on the road, grabbed him in its mouth, and ran toward the mountains. Neither the Magistrate nor the tiger was ever seen again.

That night, Da Wei was happily reunited with Lian Di.

Before many years had passed, Da Wei and Lian Di were blessed with children. As the farm prospered, Da Wei gave land to poor peasants, remembering his own suffering. He enlarged his house, adding polished redwood doors and beams and blue porcelain roof tiles. His children went to school to learn poetry and calligraphy.

Near their home, Da Wei dug a pond where Lian Di could sit and watch fish as she embroidered. Beside it, he planted a garden of bright flowers, like the ones in the mansion under the sea, and placed the rock among the flowers. Though clouds never drifted out of its holes and light never shone from the little house again, Da Wei liked to look at it and think of his father and the mansion where he had found Lian Di.

He did not need another miracle from the rock, for now he had treasures beyond his greatest hopes.

AUTHORS' NOTE

Da Wei's Treasure is adapted from a story Raymond's mother, Li Ju-fen, told her family in Shanghai. Though we have searched diligently, we have not found a printed English source for the complete tale. We believe that Raymond's mother combined elements from Pu Songling's seventeenth-century collection of magical and ghostly stories, which she knew well, with other Chinese traditional tales to create a new story. The description of the stone comes from one of Pu Songling's stories. Characters in Chinese traditional literature often find treasures beneath the sea. While Li Ju-fen must have heard a variant of the tale type called "Mysterious Housekeeper," perhaps a story similar to "The Clam Girl" found in Cora Cheney's *Tales from a Taiwan Kitchen* (New York: Dodd, Mead), portraying the wife as a transformed cat seems to be entirely her own invention.

Raymond and Margaret Chang